For Beth, Finn and Cori — D.O.
For Jessica, Axel and Raven — M.P.
For Hazel and Richard — B.M.S.

Robin Robin
This edition published in 2021 by Red Comet Press, LLC, Brooklyn, NY

Text copyright © Aardman Animations 2021
Illustrations copyright © Briony May Smith 2021
Moral rights asserted.

First published 2021 by Two Hoots an imprint of Pan Macmillan

Library of Congress Control Number: 2021942133

ISBN (HB): 978-1-63655-009-1
ISBN (Ebook): 978-1-63655-010-7

21 22 23 24 25 10 9 8 7 6 5 4 3 2 1

Manufactured in Serbia

RED
COMET
PRESS

RedCometPress.com

Aardman

Robin Robin

Written by
Dan Ojari and Mikey Please

Illustrated by
Briony May Smith

Red Comet Press • Brooklyn

Inside the egg, all was dark, but the storm was loud and close. There was a purr . . . a swoosh! The egg tumbled down, then stopped with a thump and a crack!

"What's that?" said a small voice.

"Can we eat it?" asked another.

"Of course not! It's a bird!" said a third.

"A robin, I think," said the next.

"Let's keep her," said the littlest voice yet.
"We'll call her . . . Robin."

"Chirp!" chirped Robin, flapping her wings.
She liked that idea. "Robin Robin."

Inside the burrow,
all was warm, and
the family spoke
of crumbs.

"Breadcrumbs!" whispered Dad.

"Pie crumbs!" murmured Pip.

"Cookie crumbs!" breathed Dink.

"The crumbier, the better!" chirped Robin,
as she fluffed up her feathers into two mousey ears.

The best crumbs were in the Who-man house. To get them you had to be VERY sneaky so as not to wake the Cat.

"Leave no trace, go tiptoe pace,
when sneaking into a Who-man house."

"Keep to the shadows and never be seen."

"Be quiet as a . . . MOUSE!" chirped Robin, a little too loudly.

With a CHIRP and a SMASH and a FLUTTER and a CRASH, Robin had woken the dreaded Cat.

"Don't worry," said Dad, "we'll get crumbs next time."

"You say that every time," sighed Robin.

Rumble went the bellies in the burrow that night, as the family dreamed of crumbs. But Robin was wide awake.

"I just need to be more sneaky," she chirped, slipping down from her nook in the roots and stepping out into the snow. "I'll leave no trace, go tiptoe pace. As I sneak up into the Who-man house.

"I'll keep to the shadows.
I'll never be seen,
I'LL BE QUIET AS A . . .

...CAT!"
gulped Robin.

With a CHIRP and a SMASH and a FLUTTER and a CRASH,
Robin jumped out of the back door
SMACK! into a pair of black wings.

"Oh dear," said Magpie. "Follow me!"

The birds hid in Magpie's old tree.
"What were you doing in a Who-man house?" he asked.

"Looking for crumbs," panted Robin.
"The Who-mens, they have SO many."

"The Who-mens?" said Magpie, calming himself.
"Yes . . . they have so much of everything.
And all because of the Chrim-Cross Star, hey?"

"Yes, the Chrim-Cross—WHAT?" asked Robin.

"The Chrim-Cross Star!" said Magpie, delighted.
"The Who-mens use it to get THINGS!
Once a year, they take a spikey old tree, cover it in beautiful
rubbish, put the Chrim-Cross Star on top, and make a wish!"

"Then in the morning, they get ANYTHING they want."

"Anything?" muttered Robin, dreaming of crumbs.
And right there and then, she had an idea.
"I'LL GET US THAT STAR!" chirped Robin.

"I'll leave no trace, go tiptoe pace,
when I sneak up into
the Who-man house.

"I'll keep to the
shadows, I'll never
be seen,

"HEEEELP!" chirped Robin,
above the sound of smashing and
crashing and growling, as the Cat
clawed up higher.

"FLYYYYYYY!!!" squawked Magpie.
"I can't!" chirped Robin.
"Never learned."

"Flying's easy—just flap your wings!"

And though it didn't feel like something a sneaky mouse would do, Robin raised both her wings . . . and flapped.

With a CHIRP and a SMASH and a FLUTTER and a CRASH, Robin flew out of the window!

Landing with a thump at the end of the garden, she looked back
at the mess she'd made. "I'll never be sneaky," sighed Robin.

Magpie gazed up at his Chrim-Cross Tree, now complete with a Chrim-Cross Star.
He squeezed his eyes shut and squawked to himself:
"I wish for things, the shinier the better!"

But Robin was quiet. She knew in her heart that her problems couldn't be solved with even the crumbiest of crumbs.
Right there and then, she had a better idea.

"I wish I were a REAL mouse," chirped Robin.

She squeezed her eyes shut, held her breath, and waited for her feathers to turn into paws . . .

But when she opened them again, her wings were still wings.
And there were no shiny presents for Magpie.
Maybe the Chrim-Cross Star didn't work after all.

Then Robin heard a voice. "There she is! Robin!"

Her family emerged from the brambles.

"We've been searching all night!"

"We followed the star!"

"Where have you been?" asked Dad.

Robin shuffled her feet in the snow.
"I went to get some crumbs, but I'm just no good at sneaking,"
she said. "If anything, I just draw attention to myself."

And right there and then, she had an idea . . .
"Follow me! FOLLOW ME!" chirped Robin.

Outside the Who-man house,
the mice hid in the shadows while Robin stepped
forward and cleared her throat.

Then with a CHIRP and a SMASH and a FLUTTER and a CRASH,
Robin scrambled up onto the windowsill.

"Hey, over here, look at me!" she chirped,
flapping and singing as loudly as a BIRD.

The Cat leapt up at the window to watch.
While behind her, in the shadows, the mice filled their paws.

Inside the burrow, all was well, as the
family feasted on crumbs.

"Breadcrumbs!" whispered Dad.

"Pie crumbs!" murmured Pip.

"Cookie crumbs!" breathed Dink.

"THE CRUMBIER THE BETTER," chirped Robin.